**For the Aboriginal children of Australia, who keep
the spirit of Dreamtime alive – E.M.**

To the little children – A.K.

First North American Edition

First published in Great Britain by Frances Lincoln Limited, Apollo Works,
5 Charlton Kings Road, London NW5 2SB, England.

ISBN 0-316-54314-4
Library of Congress Catalog Card Number 92-54947

10 9 8 7 6 5 4 3 2 1

Published simultaneously in Canada by Little, Brown & Company
(Canada) Limited

Printed in Hong Kong

RAINBOW BIRD

An Aboriginal Folktale from Northern Australia

by Eric Maddern
Illustrated by Adrienne Kennaway

Little, Brown and Company
Boston Toronto London

Long ago in the Time of Dreams when the world was being born, there lived a rough, tough Crocodile Man. He was huge and mean and scary, and he had one thing nobody else had.

Fire! Fire was his alone. Sometimes he held it with his foot. Sometimes he breathed it from his throat. Sometimes he balanced it on his head. He liked to play with Fire. Fire was his. Alone.

When other animals begged for Fire, Crocodile Man just laughed. If they came too close, he frightened them away, snarling and snapping his jaws.

"I'm boss for Fire," he growled through his teeth. "I'm boss for Fire!"

In a nearby tree lived Bird Woman. She could never get close to Fire. So she had no light in the dark, she was cold at night, and she ate her fish and lizards raw.

Often she pleaded with Crocodile Man for Fire, but every time he snapped back, "Eat your food raw!"

"But what about people?" Bird Woman asked sadly. "How are they to cook their food?"

"They must eat it raw, too," croaked the cross Crocodile, knocking her away with his tail. "You will not have my firesticks."

"You're so mean," sighed Bird Woman. "If I had Fire I'd share it with you." And she flew back up into the tree.

Time passed. From her tree Bird Woman watched
Crocodile Man. And she flew about, catching her food,
eating it raw, shivering with cold at night. But always
watching and waiting, waiting and watching.

Then, one afternoon . . .

Crocodile Man opened his jaws and gave the widest,
longest, sleepiest, biggest yawn anyone had ever seen.

Now's my chance, thought Bird Woman. She flashed down from the tree, snatched up the firesticks, and flew back into the air. And there was nothing Crocodile Man could do.

"Now I shall give Fire to people," said Bird Woman,
feeling proud, and she flew around the country putting
Fire into the heart of every tree.

From that day on people could make Fire using dry
sticks and logs from a tree. And they could cook their food,
keep warm at night, and light their way in the dark.

Then Bird Woman did a little dance and put the firesticks into her tail. She became the beautiful Rainbow Bird.

Now Rainbow Bird flew back to Crocodile Man.

"You must stay down there in the wet," she said. "I'll fly high in the dry. I'll be a bird. I'll stay on top. I'll live in the air. If you come up here you might die!"

And to this day Crocodile lives down in the swamp.
His Fire has gone now, but when he growls and opens
his mouth he still seems to say, "I'm boss. . . . I'm boss!"
    And Rainbow Bird? She lives in the sky, and sometimes,
if you're lucky, you can see her still taking fire to the trees
in a blaze of feathers, rainbow bright.